This Walker book belongs to:

Darcie

with love from
Granny. XXX

For Colin, Hank, and Milo Meloy, with love

First published 2015 by Walker Books Ltd, 87 Vauxhall Walk, London SE11 5HJ • This edition published 2016 • 10 9 8 7 6 5 4 3
© 2015 Carson Ellis • The right of Carson Ellis to be identified as author/illustrator of this work has been asserted by her in accordance with the
Copyright, Designs and Patents Act 1988 • This book has been hand-lettered by the author • Printed in China • All rights reserved. No part of this
book may be reproduced, transmitted or stored in an information retrieval system in any form or by any means, graphic, electronic or mechanical,
including photocopying, taping and recording, without prior written permission from the publisher. • British Library Cataloguing in
Publication Data: a catalogue record for this book is available from the British Library • ISBN 978-1-4063-6579-5 • www.walker.co.uk

Home

Carson Ellis

WALKER BOOKS
AND SUBSIDIARIES
LONDON · BOSTON · SYDNEY · AUCKLAND

Home is a house in the country.

Or home is a flat.

Some homes are boats.

Some homes are wigwams.

Some are palaces.

Or underground lairs.

Or shoes.

French people live in French homes.

Atlantians make their homes under water.

And some people live on the road.

Clean homes. Messy homes.

Tall homes.

Short homes.

Sea homes.

Bee homes.

Hollow-
tree homes.

But whose home is this?

And what about this?

Who in the world lives here?

And why?

This is the home of a Slovakian duchess.

This is the home of a Kenyan blacksmith.

This is the home of a Japanese businessman.

This is the home of a Norse god.

A babushka lives here.

A Moonian lives here.

A racoon lives here.

An artist lives here.

This is my home
and this is me.

Where is your home?
Where are you?

Carson Ellis

is the author-illustrator of the celebrated *New York Times* bestseller *Home,* her debut solo picture book, as well as being the illustrator of *The Composer Is Dead,* written by Lemony Snicket, and *Dillweed's Revenge,* written by Florence Parry Heide. She also collaborated with her husband, Colin Meloy, on the bestselling *Wildwood* series, and created the art for the albums of his band, *The Decemberists.* Carson lives with her family in Portland, USA.

Find her online at www.carsonellis.com
and on Instagram as @carsonellis.